JOISEY BOYDS

JOISEY BOYDS

The Battle for the Jersey Shore Territory

M. CHIARELLA
Illustrated by Rick Muccio

This is a fictionalized story utilizing real locations. It is not intended to give a true representation of their purpose or the people who may be connected to them.

For my son Jim who told me I had to finish, and my grandson Trevin and nephew Noah, who were my best critics.

Cast Of Main Characters

The New Jersey Tommies

Hurricane: The boss of the powerful New Jersey seagull family, the Tommies.

Mack Daddy: The head soldier of the Tommies' crew.

Goomba: The Tommie enforcer, making sure all rules and deals are followed.

Chunk, Lucky, and Crusher: Three of the Tommie crew, soldiers who want to impress their boss, Hurricane.

The Brooklyn, New York, Bennies

Bruno da Boss: The boss of the Brooklyn, New York, family, the Bennies.

Big Tuna: The head soldier of the Bennies' crew.

Tony Ravioli: The enforcer for the Bennies, making sure all rules and contracts are followed.

The Kid: A crew member who is moving up in power.

PHILLY "SHEGULLS"

Dyna and Tracy: Two resourceful female seagulls that encounter the Tommies and Bennies while on vacation.

HUMANS

Dave: A marine biologist at the Manahawkin Wildlife Refuge protecting the shore.

Jimmy: Dave's son, a curious boy seeking adventure.

Jane: The animal scientist at the Wildlife Refuge.

Natalie: The veterinarian at the Wildlife Refuge.

PROLOGUE

He hadn't been paying attention. His focus had been on getting food, but suddenly a wind gust hit him like a fist, forcing him into the ocean.

He pulled himself out and back into the air, shaking the water out of his eyes and feathers, realizing he was in trouble. He hadn't noticed how far out from shore he was, and now the wind was attacking with a heavy rage. Flooding rains began to pound him, and he was aware he was facing something bigger than an ocean squall. "Dis storm is coming heavy at me!" he thought.

The sky was gray around him, and he couldn't see the beach—he hoped it was ahead, but everything seemed turned around. The wind was pushing the rain into his eyes, and he tried to skim the water's surface to keep his direction, following the high surf that had sprung up. He thought it would take him inland.

He was beat, struggling to stay airborne, "Da shore seems like it will never happen! I wonder if I can do the distance!" He could hardly lift his wings as they beat against the storm's fury. Suddenly, a wave surged up and caught him, spinning him in its foam and finally throwing him onto the beach. He opened his eyes to see another huge wave getting ready to sock him, and he pushed himself back up into the air, trying to get farther up the beach.

The wind and rain were tossing him in all directions like he was a ball in a football game. He was squinting to try to improve his vision when he saw a darker patch up ahead. What was dat? *Slam!* He was thrown into rocks and fell back to the beach. "Man! Dose rocks gave me a one-two punch!" He tried to just lie there, but even though the rocks blocked some of the wind, the rain was as fierce as ever.

He dragged his body up, trying to find a space in the rocks where he could protect himself from the storm and unexpectedly fell into an opening that he realized was a cave. It hit him: he was safe from the terror attacking his beach, and he allowed himself to rest. He felt beat up, a stabbing agony attacked his body and exhaustion overwhelmed him. "I was right, dat storm did a numbah on me," he thought as he passed out.

He came to a little while later, full of pain, and lay listening—to nothing! He realized the storm must be over, and he slowly picked himself up off the cave floor. He gave himself the old heave-ho, pushing his body outside. His right wing dragged oddly on the sand. He walked past the rocks surrounding the cave and tried to lift off over the beach so he could see where he was.

With a loud squawking cry, he fell back down and knew his wing was broken. He used his beak to push himself upright and struggled farther toward the ocean, finally collapsing again. The sun had come back out and was beating down on him, draining away his strength. His eyes closed.

He felt his body being lifted and a sharp sting in his side. His eyes flew open, and he saw a human in a white coat. The human had pushed something sharp into him. "Dis is trouble! Dis guy's trying to ambush me!" He started to struggle against the human but felt the hand around him tighten as the human gently examined his broken wing and then placed him in a cage.

The human carried him down the beach to a boat, and they followed the coast south. He closed his eyes, trying to control his fear. The human took the cage off the boat and into a building, setting it on a white table.

Next, the human took him out and placed a metal band on his leg.

The human gave him another sharp shot, and he felt himself relax and then he slept. When he woke his wing didn't hurt, but he couldn't move it. He was in a larger cage with food and water, and he leaned in to take a big drink. Looking around, he saw other cages with animals in them and assumed they had all gotten pinched—sent to this jail—by the human. Then he noticed writing on the wall: M-A-N-A-H-A-W-K-I-N. "Manahawkin. What's dat?" he wondered.

The days passed, and he saw other humans in white coats. They all treated him gently, and there was no shortage of food or water. Soon he trusted the humans and stopped trying to peck or bite them.

Finally a day came when he was put back on the white table. They cut the tapes holding his wing and stepped away from him. Carefully he stretched the wing out, and then lightly flapped both wings.

The human spoke to him. "Well, you are one strong, tough guy—surviving a storm like that. We've logged you into our books as 'Hurricane.'" The human walked over and opened a door. "Go ahead," he told him. "You can find your way."

Hurricane flew out the door and was soon in the soft ocean wind heading home to Toms River. He flapped his healed wing, testing its strength, and thought, "Dose humans saved my life!" He soared higher, happy to have his freedom, and laughed to himself, "Hurricane—dat's a name I can live wit'."

Meet The Boss

On a beautiful morning at Seaside Heights on the Jersey Shore, the ocean was rolling in with mild waves, the sky was a cloudless blue, and the sun was creating the perfect day for swimming.

The beach was crowded with towels, blankets, beach chairs, umbrellas, and—most importantly—food. The food was packaged in many types of containers: coolers, baskets, bags, and shiny foil packages.

The bright colors of foil bags, sparkling and reflecting the sun, lay on a blanket like an open invitation. Inside these bags a bird could find chips, crackers, cookies, or candy.

Suddenly, bird shadows appeared on the sand. A moment later, the shadows disappeared and three seagulls landed near the blanket. They split up, casually hopping around the area, watching the blanket closely.

The three gulls were members of the New Jersey family, the Tommies. Toms River, New Jersey, was the gang's hometown. The Tommies acted as protection for Toms River, making it one of the safest towns for birds in the country, but in summer it was profitable for the Tommies to leave their little town and fly closer to the Shore. Seaside Heights Beach was the piece of the Shore the Tommies claimed as their own, including all the food the tourists brought.

"Hey, boys!" said a bird with one eye that drooped nearly closed. He was called Lucky because he had survived a run-in with a seagull from the New York family, the Bennies. "This looks like it's gonna be a great summa!"

"Yeah, how'd ya know that, Lucky?" screeched a larger bird named Crusher. "Ya haven't been able to see straight since that Benny gotcha!"

"Ech! Those New Yorkas! If those Bennies turn up this year, I'll show 'em!" Lucky raised his wing and brushed his eye. He remembered the bird who had nearly taken his eye out—Tony Ravioli, the enforcer for the Bennies.

Lucky could almost see Tony Ravioli coming at him again, as his memory took him back to the fight with the Bennies last summer. The force of the blow had knocked Lucky down, blinded from the blood running into his eye. Tony Ravioli had flown away, leaving Lucky lying on the beach.

"Ya can count on me to help ya, Lucky. They don't call me Crusher for nothin'! I'll help ya crush those Bennies—I didn't fly down here from Toms River just for food!"

"Well, I did!" squawked Chunk, a round gull waddling toward them. "Ya want some lunch or what?" The birds' attention focused again on the blanket full of food.

"Let me go in for it," said Crusher. "I'm the fastest."

"Yeah, but I'm the hungriest!" With that, Chunk dived at the blanket and stole a bag. He flew off toward a clear area of the beach and started attacking the foil with his beak. Crusher flew down next to him, grabbed one of the bag's corners in his beak, and the two gulls pulled against each other in a tug-of-war.

The bag ripped open, and chips spilled out over the sand. "Chips! My favorite!" yelled Chunk, and the three birds began devouring the chips. Soon they were joined by more birds trying to get to the food, including some just passing through the area—egrets, terns, and other seagulls.

"This ain't enough! I definitely need a bigga supply!" whooped Chunk. He took off toward the blankets, flying low and swooping in to grab another shiny bag lying open near a human on a beach chair.

"Hey, drop that!" yelled the human, nearly falling over as he tried to get out of his chair to stop the gull. Chunk was a Laughing Gull, and he screeched out his high-pitched laugh at the man—"Ha ha ha!"—as he flew back to his friends.

Chunk felt even hungrier after the excitement of gathering the food right out from under the human's nose. "Cookies—great!" he said. He began to shake the bag.

Something made him look up. It's then he realized the beach had gone quiet. Standing in front of him was a huge, Great Black-Backed gull, the boss of the family, with his two bodyguards, Mack Daddy and Goomba, who were also Great Black-Backed gulls.

"H-h-hey, Hurricane," Chunk stuttered. "Whatsa story? Ya want some lunch?"

"Well, guys," snarled Hurricane, "ain't this nice. Chunk here is offering me lunch!" Hurricane's big webbed foot stomped on the cookie bag. "These cookies just became mine! Not because I want 'em, but because I can take 'em. You're just one of my soldiers, Chunk. What you better be givin' me is respect or ya gonna find yourself in isolation—I'll make sure no boyds hang out wit' ya."

Chunk looked down at Hurricane's foot and noticed the shiny metal band around his leg. He remembered the story about that metal band: the big gull had gotten caught in a huge storm, and some humans had found him lying on the beach with his wing broken. They took the gull with them and fixed his wing, attaching the band around his leg at the same time.

The humans had released him, and he flew back to Toms River. That's when he got the name Hurricane and became head of the gang. Any bird who could survive a storm like that had to be the strongest. There was writing on the metal band: "Manahawkin WMA." Rumor had it that Manahawkin was the head of all the seagull families.

Chunk slowly backed away, his head lowered with the respect that Hurricane demanded.

Hurricane began eating cookies out of the bag. Mack Daddy and Goomba darted at the other birds on the beach, keeping them away from the boss.

Chunk circled around and slid next to his two buddies, Crusher and Lucky. "Geez, Chunk! That was close! Ya know we gotta keep Hurricane happy. Ya should have just backed away as soon as ya saw him—let him have *all* the food if he wants," peeped Lucky.

"I couldn't think!" said Chunk. "He always scares me."

"He scares all of us," whispered Crusher. "That's why he's the boss. But that's a good idea, Lucky! C'mon, let's get Hurricane some more food, and he'll know we respect him."

The three seagulls lifted up on the ocean breeze and went out to raid more blankets.

5

Hit The Shore

It was hot in Bath Beach, Brooklyn: 98 degrees hot. The original beach had been paved over to make the Shore Parkway. Now the leaves were wilted, the grass was brown, and the air was sticky: the local seagulls were feeling all of it.

Four gulls were perched on the Bay Parkway sign to see if they could catch a breeze. Their beaks were hanging open to release the heat out of their bodies. Bruno da Boss, Tony Ravioli, Big Tuna, and the Kid were all members of the Brooklyn family, the Bennies—with Bruno da Boss running the show. Bruno was a large Herring Gull.

Big Tuna, also a Herring Gull, was Bruno's "Capo," the head of the family's crew. Tony Ravioli was the enforcer, and the Kid, a smaller Mew Gull, was one of the crew soldiers.

"What yooze guys want to do?" asked Big Tuna as he opened and closed his wings trying to keep cool. "There's a baseball game going on over on Benson Avenue, or we could go over to Coney Island and eat some hot dogs."

"Fugget about it!" hissed Bruno. "Whadda ya think this is, a Nathan's hot dog eatin' contest?"

"Let's go over to the Pizza Den and see what's in the trash," panted Tony Ravioli. He loved to eat anything Italian.

"Whatsa matta wit' ya!" Bruno shot his wing open and knocked Tony off the sign. "This city stinks of trash. Look, they're haulin' some away down there. That's the trouble: Brooklyn's hot and it stinks. We need to get outta town and find some fresh air and good eats. We're going down the Jersey Shore."

The other three birds snapped their beaks shut, surprise showing in their eyes. "Wow, boss!" said Big Tuna. "I thought you was just gonna tell us to find some lemon ice or somethin'. I never thought of goin' to the Jersey Shore. I'd love to chase some of those Tommies."

"That's right, guys! We might as well have ourselves a little fun while we cool off at the beach. I'd like to meet up wit' dat Hurricane again. I got some stuff to settle wit' dat wiseguy. Kid, go get the rest of the gang and catch up to us."

Bruno took off with Big Tuna and Tony Ravioli. Kid alerted the rest of the family, and soon a flock of sixteen gulls were headed toward Seaside Heights in New Jersey. As the sun came up over the Atlantic Ocean the next morning, the Bennies landed on the beach at Seaside Heights.

"I ask ya," said Bruno da Boss, "ain't this better than being a 'corner man' in Brooklyn—just sittin' 'round on a corner watchin' the world go by?"

"Yeah," replied Tony Ravioli. "I betcha dollars to doughnuts we're gonna be eatin' good today!"

"Aaah, ya knucklehead, all ya do is talk food. I'm lookin' for more action than that. I wanna find those Tommies. This year we're takin' over their beach!" With that, Bruno waved Big Tuna over.

"Go find out where that Hurricane is hangin'," he told Big Tuna.

Big Tuna flew down the beach where he saw a little Blue Heron fishing in the ocean. "Hiya," Tuna said to the heron. "Ya seen any of those Tommies around?"

"Tommies?" questioned the heron.

"Yeah, ya know, that gull Hurricane and his group—ya seen them?"

"Oh, Hurricane. Everybody knows Hurricane around here! Dontcha know they all go back to Toms River at night? They'll be showin' up."

"Tanks!" said Big Tuna. He flew back and reported to Bruno da Boss what he had learned.

"OK," yelped Bruno to his Bennies. "Go ahead and get somethin' to eat while the coast is clear. Tony, find me what I would like for my breakfast. I'm gonna find us a base."

The gulls separated, looking for food. Only a few tourists were on the beach this early, walking or running, so there were no foil bags around. Tony spotted some sea turtle eggs hidden in the sand, and he swooped down and grabbed a couple for Bruno.

Seaside Heights has two fun spots. One is the FunTown Pier, with a boardwalk and amusement rides. The other spot is the Casino Pier, attached to a water park.

Aromas from the pizza shops, sausage stands, and cotton candy machines tempt everybody's taste buds— including the seagulls! Bruno could smell all of it, as he looked down at the humans opening their stands.

Bruno set up watch on the FunTown Pier, and Tony deposited the eggs in front of him. Bruno nodded at him. "You're a good earner, Ravioli." Then he turned to watch the beach again. Tony joined the other gulls, skimming low over the ocean, catching fresh fish.

High up in the air, a single Laughing Gull was flying. Chunk had come down from Toms River to the beach early, to get more food. He noticed all the activity of gulls fishing and knew he had to check it out. He saw the Sky Ride was shut down, so he flew to the top to get a better view.

His eyes searched the beach, trying to figure out whether he knew any of the seagulls. Suddenly he spotted the large gull sitting on the pier. "Bruno da Boss and the Bennies! When they're around it's nothin' but bad news. I gotta warn Hurricane!"

At the same moment, Bruno looked up and saw Chunk. He blared a command at Tony Ravioli, and Tony took off toward Chunk. "I'm gonna hafta do the Jersey shuffle and fly outta here fast!" Chunk thought. "Sometimes I wish I didn't like to eat so much. This belly's in my way."

Chunk flew off the Sky Ride and over the Saltwater Taffy shack. He looked back and saw Tony Ravioli getting closer. "I think that's the guy that hit Lucky's eye." For once Chunk was glad he was a smaller gull. He floated in and out of attractions, finally losing Tony in the antique carousel.

He straightened out his flight pattern and headed back toward Toms River. When he got to the town, he spotted his family hanging out in the parking lot of Toms River Diner. He threw himself on the ground in front of Hurricane, which caused Mack Daddy and Goomba to grab his wings and toss him away.

"B-b-b-bennies!" Chunk gasped from his laid-out position on the ground. "Bruno da Boss!"

Suddenly, Hurricane was standing over him, his large, hooked beak nearly in his eye. "Where?" he blared at Chunk.

"Seaside!" Chunk choked out.

Hurricane turned toward his gang. "Bruno—him I been waitin' for! Let's go. We're gonna do a number on those Bennies!"

The gang cheered, and quickly twenty gulls were in the air. A short time later, the group was hovering over Seaside Heights. Hurricane spotted Bruno da Boss before any of the Benny family spotted the Tommies, and he dove straight at him, scaring him off his perch.

Bruno flew straight up, chest-bumping Mack Daddy out of his way. Big Tuna and Tony Ravioli were quickly flying next to him, and then Bruno and Hurricane were hovering eye to eye.

The other seagulls noticed the action, and the Tommies and Bennies began dividing up behind their bosses, as if an invisible line were in the sky. Humans were running and screaming as the birds flew at each other, thinking they were being dive-bombed by the gulls.

"Let's take this somewheres private!" Hurricane snarled at Bruno.

Brooklyn Boyds Mean Trouble!

The birds followed Hurricane inland to a parking lot between the piers. They regrouped and began to fight—swarming at each other, tearing out feathers, pecking, and screeching with sharp cries.

Hurricane and Bruno faced off, and the other gulls stopped to watch. The enforcers of each family paced around the two bosses, darting at any bird that stepped too close.

Hurricane and Bruno's hooked beaks locked as they each tried to stop the other from biting. Hurricane beat his longer wings against Bruno, slapping at his head. Bruno kicked at Hurricane's stomach with his large webbed feet, making it difficult for Hurricane to breathe. Hurricane grabbed Bruno's neck with his beak and flipped him over on the ground.

There was a loud whistling and squawking coming from all the other gulls. Planting his foot on Bruno's chest, Hurricane looked up. Bruno wiggled out from where he

lay pinned to the ground and looked to see what the gulls were making noise about.

Two seagull hens had landed in the parking lot. One of the girls was beautiful, with a shiny black head that was not usually seen at the shore.

Hurricane looked at Bruno as he heard him join in the whistling. He realized they couldn't continue the fight in front of the girls.

He flared his wings at Bruno. "Listen, ya goon, I'm gonna let ya go for now. But you better stick around, cuz we're gonna finish this."

"Who do ya think ya are, tryin' to tell me what will be?" Bruno came back.

"I'm the boyd who says how things go around here!" Hurricane replied. "And this does not go down now. You can take your crew and hang out at the Casino Pier. But this vacation ain't for free. Your boys hafta wet my beak. You find any good food action, ya better make sure I get my share!"

He noticed the two "she-gulls" had gotten close and were starting to listen to the conversation. Quickly, he finished it up. "So, Bruno pal, I'll be seeing ya around."

"Yeah," Bruno said, glancing at the new gulls. "Yooze will be seeing me for sure—and real soon!"

"I'll be watchin' ya—I mean for ya." Hurricane responded, and then turned smoothly to the two gullettes. "Hey, ladies, you must be from out of town. What brought ya down the shore?"

"Yo, boys! My name's Tracy, and this is my BFF, Dyna. We're from south Philly, on vacation." Tracy was a Black-legged Kittiwake gull, and the guys couldn't help noticing how pretty she looked with her soft, fluffy gray and white feathers. "Look, Dyna. I think we got us a couple of ath-a-letes."

"Yooze from Philadelpia, huh? Hey, hon, let me take you two girls somewhere we can talk and all of us get to know each other. You're in Jersey now. Ya know what they say—in Jersey we don't pump our gas, we pump our fists. I can protect ya from this Benny New York trash." Hurricane gestured at Bruno da Boss.

"Don't pay attention to dat guy," Bruno retorted, pointing at Hurricane. "He's got more hot air to dish out than I have feathers on my head. Ya wants protection, I'm the guy who can guarantee it."

"There's definitely some attitude on this beach, Tracy," Dyna said. "They think they're the boss all right. They're actin' like they're Bruce Springsteen or somebody. Let's get outta this parkin' lot and head over to the water."

Dyna's shiny black feathers framed her dark eyes, fluffing slightly in the ocean breeze as she gave the two bosses a cool look. She was small and dainty, and as she turned to fly away, Hurricane noticed the dark gray under her wings. "Sweeet!" he thought.

"Oh, Dyna's just upset cuz I come up here instead of goin' to Atlantic Ciddy," said Tracy. "I got an idea you'll see us around. We can talk then!" She winked and followed Dyna, who was heading for the beach.

"That girl is mine," said Bruno, and he took off after them. Hurricane responded by jetting up into Bruno's flight path and knocking him back.

"I suggest ya don't do that," Hurricane scowled at Bruno. "I told ya, take your crew over to the Casino Pier."

Bruno's gulls swarmed forward. Bruno stretched his wings out to stop them. "It's OK, boys. We don't want no trouble." Bruno led the flock of gulls toward the Casino Pier.

"That was too easy. Bruno's up to somethin'," Hurricane told Mack Daddy as his gang landed back on the beach. "Chunk! Get over here!"

Chunk froze where he stood between Lucky and Crusher. He looked at both of them, and then slowly started moving toward Hurricane, wondering what he had done wrong. His two friends followed as close as they dared.

"What're we gonna do if they hurt Chunk?" Lucky whispered to Crusher.

"We'll just hafta try and grab Chunk and head for the water." Crusher answered. "Maybe we can lose Hurricane and find a place to hide."

"Ya mean run off?" Lucky questioned.

"Yeah," said Crusher. "We gotta do what we gotta do for a stand-up guy like Chunk."

"Chunk! Don't take all summa," Hurricane snapped. "Yeah, that's OK, bring your buddies."

The three birds stood in front of Hurricane and his two bodyguards, Mack Daddy and Goomba. The three friends tried to look big and tough, but they were all shaking.

"G-g-gee boss, ya really did a number on that Bruno," said Chunk.

"Yeah, right, whatevah," said Hurricane, brushing off the compliment. "Look, yooze guys are part of my crew, and I have a job for ya." Hurricane looked at each bird separately. "Yooze three know the beach, the boardwalk, the piers, and ya ain't much to look at. Nobody's gonna notice ya. I want you to stay close to the Casino Pier and the Bennies."

"You!" he pointed at Lucky. "Don't let Tony Ravioli see ya. He might remember givin' you that eye. Do you three unnerstan? I want ya to tail those Bennies and spill everything ya see directly to me."

The three birds just nodded their heads together, looking a little like bobble heads.

"Now remember, yooze're Tommies! We have a Code of Silence. If you get caught by the Bennies, ya better not rat on the family or I'll find you—personally. Got it?"

"Sure, Hurricane, we'll keep our beaks shut. We're your guys," Chunk replied, taking the lead of the three.

Hurricane gave each of them one more look, and then signaled to Mack Daddy and Goomba that it was time to head back to Toms River.

Chunk, Lucky, and Crusher were alone in the parking lot. "Wow, this is big. We hafta make sure we do this right," gasped Lucky.

"Yeah right, let's take a cruise and see if we can come up with a plan," said Chunk, taking charge. "Lucky, you take the beach and FunTown. Crusher and I'll fly over da Casino Pier. We'll meet ya back at the FunTown Pier."

"Who died and made yooze boss, Chunk?" squawked Lucky.

"Well, those Bennies know what ya look like, Lucky. They're gonna be watchin' for Hurricane to start makin' moves," said Chunk.

"Yeah, Lucky, we gotta figure out what's up. Chunk and me'll make the first pass over the Casino, meet back up wit'

ya, and then we can make a plan." Crusher put his wing over Lucky's shoulders. "We're all in this together."

"OK, let's get goin' before its dark," agreed Lucky.

Every Which Way

The Casino Pier in Seaside Heights was amazing. There were rides, arcades, miniature golf, and—most importantly—food. Hurricane had sent Bruno da Boss and the Bennies there, hoping the food would keep them busy and off his beach until he had time to deal with them.

Bruno set up headquarters at the rooftop miniature golf course on the boardwalk. This location gave him the best view of the area to watch for any Tommies and any action. The boardwalk was where most of the food stands were located, so his soldiers would stay happy. Big Tuna, Tony Ravioli, and the Kid were sitting on the edge of the roof with him.

Bruno's headquarter strategy did not stop Big Tuna from asking questions. "Boss—put us wise—why did you let that Hurricane knock ya down?"

Bruno looked at the three members of his crew and started laughing. "I ask ya, I was good, right? That Hurricane,

he don't know from nothin'. I just bought us time. We're gonna take to the mattresses, and we have to find a place to set up. I'm gonna own this beach, and if it means war with those Tommies, we're the birds that can bring it on."

The three family members gave their respects to their leader.

"Oh, sure, boss. I was just goofin' on ya. I saw yooze was in control."

"Yeah, boss, I knows ya gonna burn that Hurricane," Tony Ravioli put in.

"Nobody can scam those Tommies like you can, boss," chimed in the Kid.

"Enough, ya losers!" Bruno came back at them. "Now get off this tar rooftop and head for the beach. Here's the plan. Kid, get us a steady food supply away from this pier. We need some backup supplies.

"Tuna, find us some places we can hole up—we need a lotta hideouts to keep those Tommies guessin'.

"Ravioli, you're the enforcer—get out and enforce! Take some of the crew and set up watch points. Report back here at dark. Me, I'm gonna find those two dolls from earlier."

The seagulls took off on their missions, none of them noticing Chunk and Crusher hiding in the arcade. Big Tuna sent several soldiers to guard Bruno.

"You're bigga than me, Crusher. Ya better follow Big Tuna. I don't think I could handle him. I'll take the Kid," said Chunk.

"What about Bruno da Boss? How we gonna cover him?"

"There are too many Bennies for just us three. We'll just hafta let Bruno go. Bruno and his guards are big, and shadowin' them doesn't sound smart. Our job is to get information safely back to Hurricane. We can let Hurricane know we could use more guys."

"OK," replied Crusher. "I'll meet up with you and Lucky at the FunTown Pier like we planned." The two birds left each other to take care of business.

At that moment, Lucky was flying over the general Seaside Heights beach area. He saw a few of the Bennies fishing in the ocean, but it didn't look as though there was anything threatening going on. He also saw the two she-gulls from earlier at the parking-lot fight. He landed on the beach to see better.

"Yeah," he thought to himself, "those two girls are real lookers." He knew the girls were out of his league, but he still couldn't help watching them. They were so pretty.

Tracy and Dyna were charming the tourists, targeting the children. Dyna's black feathers were attracting attention since she was the only seagull with a shiny black head. The girls worked as a team. Tracy flew in little trick loop-de-loops to entertain the children, as Dyna hopped closer, being friendly with the kids so they could get a better look at her.

They were rewarded with choice bits of food, sandwiches, brownies, cookies, and more. Lucky was impressed by their skill and forgot for a minute why he was on the beach—until he saw one of Bruno's crew land close by. Lucky took off with a loud flapping of wings. Anxious to avoid being recognized, he flew out over the edge of the ocean.

Soon the rest of Bruno's guards landed, forming a line in front of Tracy and Dyna. Puzzled, the two girls turned toward them just as Bruno da Boss himself touched down. Bruno swaggered over, his soldiers parting to let him through.

"Hey, how ya doin', chickies?" Bruno nodded as he greeted Tracy and Dyna. "Jeetjet?"

"Whaaat?" questioned Tracy.

"Uh, da boss is asking you did ya eat yet," interpreted one of the crew.

"Yeah," said Bruno. "I was lookin' to take yooze two dolls to eat. I got my guys lookin' for a hash house. Whadda ya say?"

"You guys," sighed Dyna, "always thinkin' we'd go to some joint wit' ya. First, we ain't no chickies. Second, me

23

an' Tracy got enuff sugah here." She pointed at the kids waiting to give them food. "Right, Tracy?"

"Yeah, those humans are feedin' us fine," said Tracy, reaching up with her wing to fluff her head feathers. "We're here vacationin'. We didn't ask nothin' from nobody. We got our own plans to head over to the piers later to find some music or see if the Philly's game is on someplace."

"Yooze like baseball, huh?" observed Bruno. "I could meet ya and hook you up with da game."

"Hey! The Phils were the champions of National League Baseball last year! We Phillies don't need to get hooked up. We can take care of ourselves. C'mon, Tracy, let's get a change of scene."

The two girls picked up and flew over to a blanket of humans who were eating from a large cooler. It didn't take long before the humans were feeding them, too.

Lucky had heard and seen everything from his location on some pilings. He watched Bruno da Boss and his crew fly off and decided it was time to head over to the FunTown Pier to meet up with Chunk and Crusher.

Crusher was trying to follow Big Tuna on the sly, not sure what the large seagull was up to, but keeping himself alert in case he had to be ready to fight. Big Tuna stopped to speak to one of his soldiers:

"Hey, you! Skinny Molink!" He pointed at a skinny bird. "Com'ere, we got a job."

The skinny bird actually looked excited as he came up to Big Tuna. "Capo!" the bird said, giving Big Tuna his family title.

"Shut your beak! I don't wanna be talkin' with ya. I hafta go target some places for us to hole up, and I want you to make a memory of 'em. I'm putting you in charge of showing the crew where they can hide out. Ya get this right, and I'll promote yooze."

Crusher had jumped back into the arcade to hide and was glad he had, since he could hear the conversation. He let the two seagulls get a head start on him and then followed at a distance, making note of every location where he saw Big Tuna nodding his head and gesturing to Skinny. There were eight spots in all.

Feeling pretty good at his success, Crusher headed to the FunTown Pier to meet the other guys.

Meanwhile, Chunk didn't know that Bruno had given the Kid a mission close to his heart—looking for food locations. Chunk knew almost all of the best locations on the beach, and as he followed the Kid, he guessed at what the Kid's mission was.

Chunk tailed the Kid outside the Casino Pier, and then watched as the Kid went over to the boardwalk. He saw

him land and walk into some of Chunk's favorite places where there was pizza, sausage, and more.

Next, the Kid headed for the Casino Pier Beach and started skimming the water close to the shore. Often he would dive down to look at the shore itself.

After a little while, Chunk was surprised to see the Kid land, and Chunk flew higher up on the beach so that he wouldn't be seen. He noticed the area where the Kid landed was a salt marsh that Chunk had never noticed before.

The Kid was sampling some kind of food out of the marsh area, but it was small enough that Chunk couldn't tell what it was. Soon the Kid started flying back toward the pier beach, and Chunk flew down toward the marsh to see what the Kid found so interesting.

Chunk saw the marsh had a colony of marine snails. "These look delicious!" he thought. "I'll bring the guys back to try them out." But first, he knew he had to finish his mission, so he took off after the Kid.

Once Chunk confirmed that the Kid had returned to Bruno and the Bennies, he went to meet Lucky and Crusher on the FunTown Pier.

"Whoa!" Chunk whooped as he listened to Lucky and Crusher's information. "I think that's off the hook! We done better than I ever knew. Let's get to Hurricane to make our report."

Hurricane and the Tommies were back at the Toms River Diner. Hurricane, Mack Daddy, and Goomba listened to the three soldiers' information. Hurricane even laughed at Lucky's report of how the two Philadelphia females had shot down Bruno's dinner invitation.

"Those girls are the bomb. We gotta get ta know 'em better. So, what's up with that Tony Ravioli, Bruno's enforcer?"

"W-w-well, s-s-see, uh, w-w-we couldn't follow him. We didn't have enough guys. Tony was the mug who done Lucky's eye. We thought he might recognize us, so we let him slide." Chunk was looking at Hurricane's feet while he spoke, and he snuck a look at his face to see if Hurricane looked angry.

Mack Daddy sneered at the crew. "Those guys are scared of that sap, Tony? He's a piece a cake. Let me give him a shakedown."

Hurricane walked thoughtfully back and forth in front of Lucky, Chunk, and Crusher. He stopped in front of them and began talking. "This is very encouraging, boys. Yooze are on ya way to promotion—I'm thinkin' ya keep this up, you could become top guys."

Hurricane looked at Mack Daddy. "I shoulda given 'em more guys, Mack. They was goin' every which way with only three of 'em. Yooze is right. That Tony Ravioli needs a shakedown, Mack, and you is the guy to do dat. It's getting dark, so let's get the crew together for a meetin' at sunrise. We meet here."

With that, the small group broke up, and Chunk, Crusher, and Lucky puffed out their chests a little farther after Hurricane's approval. "Did ya hear that? We hafta be here first thing, up front, so we can be part of Hurricane's plan for tomorrow," Chunk said. He hooked a wing around each of his buddies as they headed to the roof of the diner to spend the night.

Going To The Mattresses

The sun could not rise fast enough for both the Tommies and the Bennies. The two families were hyped up and thinking the same thing: war—going to the mattresses. Hurricane was bringing his crew to the Toms River Diner parking lot, and Bruno da Boss had his outfit back at the Seaside rooftop miniature golf area, which was closed and empty that early in the morning.

"Yooze know what this is about. We are goin' ta war! We're gonna take this beach and make it ours. Those Tommies will be givin' their summer control to us."

Bruno looked out at his crew. "The Kid found us food. Big Tuna found us places to hide. Tony Ravioli drew a picture of all the locations ovah there in that sand trap. I want yooze to look at it and remember all of 'em. Skim over the areas and look at 'em. Then you are gonna follow the Kid to the food stops. Hideouts and food could help keep us alive."

He glared at the seagulls circled around him. "I'm not losing this thing because of some idiot, get me? I want you to know this stuff through and through. Now we meets back here in two hours, and I'll put ya wise to my plan. If yooze are late, I'll have ya chased outta this family."

Over at the Toms River Diner parking lot, Hurricane and the Tommies were having their meeting.

"Good to see ya, boys! Looks like everybody's here and as ready as me to get into this thing with dose Bennies. Mack Daddy, ya know what I want. I wants Tony Ravioli outta the picture! I wanna know what he knows. Figure out a trap for that goon. Enforcer against enforcer."

"Goomba, you is gonna be my underboss for this operation. Split the guys up and give 'em jobs. I want every Benny goon tailed. We need some defenses, so you better take care of that, too."

Then Hurricane turned toward Chunk, Lucky, and Crusher. "You three!" The three soldiers straightened up as Hurricane looked at them. "Yooze are a special team reportin' only to me. I want ya on Big Tuna and the Kid night and day till we finish this thing up. I wanna know everythin'. Unnerstand?"

"Yeah, boss," the three birds said in harmony.

"I wanna make one thing clear." Hurricane glared at all his crew. "Bruno da Boss is mine. We got unfinished bizness. He'll be expectin' me to deliver a personal message. And number two—yooze better all keep clean! I don't want no snitches in my outfit! Bruno'll be tryin' to have you shadowed, too. Now all of ya—be back this afternoon to report."

Hurricane signaled to four soldiers to follow him, and he took wing. Chunk looked at Lucky and Crusher. "Well, I can take the Kid. Since ya followed him yesterday, Crusher, you two see if yooze can find Big Tuna." During the past days, Chunk had become the leader of the three friends. "I'm gonna take a look down by the water."

"Sure, Chunk," Crusher said. "I think we'll try to find Big Tuna back by da arcade."

"OK. We know the Kid is in charge of food, and the Tuna has got the hideouts. But what do they got goin' on today? Let's use the mornin' to figgah dat out. We can meet for lunch at the FunTown Pier. It worked pretty good yestaday, huh?"

"Sounds good, Chunk. Come on, Crusher, let's race over." Lucky and Crusher took off, and Chunk headed for the beach.

Hurricane was out cruising Seaside Heights—his beach. He laughed to himself. "Dose Bennies—New Yorkas— thinkin' they could take my beach over." Looking down, he saw the two pretty girls from Philadelphia skimming over the water, catching fish. "Well, there's Dyna! I haven't found any hen that interestin' for a long time."

He signaled to his bodyguards and flew down next to Dyna, who looked up from the ocean in surprise. "Whatsa

31

story?" Hurricane asked her. "Wanna head ovah to da beach and talk, hon?"

"My name's not 'hon,'" she answered.

"Oh, come on, Dyna!" whined Tracy flying up on Dyna's other side. "I'm tired. Let's go hit the beach."

Dyna did not say anything, but she did change her flight pattern toward the shore. Hurricane's soldiers followed them closely.

"So, what've ya got?" Dyna said to Hurricane, as the three birds landed.

He strutted over to one of the blankets and stole a bag of cookies, bringing the bag to the two girls and ripping it open. "Sweets for da sweets," he said.

"Oooh," said Tracy. "Dessert!" She started eating the cookies as Hurricane and Dyna gave each other the once over.

Dyna had to admit that Hurricane was a strong, handsome-looking gull. He also showed a powerful personality that she liked.

Hurricane found something in Dyna that made him want to protect her, even though he could tell she was a fighter. Her small size made her look beautiful and delicate.

"I guess we could use some company," Dyna told Hurricane. "We was a little bored yestaday. Maybe ya knows somewhere we could getta sandwich later."

"A sandwich would be great!" Tracy chipped in. She always liked to talk about food.

"Yeah," Hurricane answered. "Later would be good. Maybe ya'd like to try some Joisey pizza 'stead of a sandwich. I'll meet you girls right back here at dinner time and escort ya." Hurricane looked only at Dyna as he said this, and she looked back with her beak slightly open in a small smile.

Hurricane and his crew flew off toward the Casino Pier, leaving the two girls to the beautiful summer day. Hurricane realized that hoping to see Dyna again was the main reason he had started his search for Bruno da Boss at the beach. He was looking forward to seeing her again at dinner.

Farther down the beach, Chunk was also cruising along the shore, looking for the Kid. He had an idea that he might find him at the salt marsh. As he got closer to the marsh, he saw a flock of six gulls feeding there, but did not see the Kid among them. Since he didn't recognize any of them, he thought he would land and see what was going on.

Although all of the gulls looked up when Chunk landed, the chubby little gull did not seem a threat, so they went back to their eating and talking.

"I ask ya, did the Kid hook us up or what?" a black-legged gull asked. "We got some crabs, some crayfish, and these tasty munchies." He held up a sea snail in his beak, then he snapped it shut over the snail.

"Yeah," answered another. "But I'm missin' those hero subs in da trash back in Brooklyn. How long is da boss keepin' us here? This don't seem like no vacation."

A yellow-legged gull responded, "I heard we was makin' a move tonight against those Tommies and dat Hurricane goon. Bruno is gonna tell us at the meetin'."

"What're we waitin' for? Let's get back there!"

Chunk watched in amazement as the flock of Bennies took off toward the piers. He thought about what they had said and realized Hurricane would want to know that the Bennies were moving on him tonight. He was hoping Lucky and Crusher were gaining more information by following Big Tuna.

Chunk decided to head back to the FunTown Pier to look for the Kid and see if he could meet up early with his friends. But first he had to sample some of this delicious food living in the marsh!

Chunk was just finishing up a crayfish and reaching for a sea snail when a large bird buzzed his head, forcing him to hug the ground. He looked up and saw Tony Ravioli, Bruno da Boss's enforcer. Chunk could not stop the shaking that was taking over his body.

"Hi, ya," Tony said, as he watched Chunk pick himself up. "I was just goofin' on ya. I thought yooze was one of those Tommies but"—and Tony pointed at the way Chunk was shaking—"I see I was mistakin'." Tony started chuckling as he turned his back. "Now go see where you gotta go. Get outta here and leave me to enjoy my meal." Tony started eating the sea snails.

Chunk pulled himself up as tall as his small body would let him, and his shaking stopped. A hard look came into his normally kind eyes, and his voice came out with an edge of steel. "Yeah, I'm done here. I'm goin'. But I got a feelin' we'll be meetin' up somewhere later, and I'll be givin' ya a goofin' you won't forget."

The surprisingly strong voice that came out of Chunk made Tony look around startled as he watched Chunk leave. He wondered if he had made a mistake about the round gull. Maybe he had been a Tommy. But the food took his attention back, and he forgot all about Chunk.

Hurricane was a large and strong seagull. He stood nearly three feet tall, and his wingspan was over five feet. When Hurricane left Dyna and Tracy, he soared high, higher than his bodyguards could follow him and he lifted out of the normal seagull traffic.

From that height, Hurricane could see everything happening at seaside—both the Casino and FunTown piers

and most of the beach areas. The most important thing was that no one was looking for him up that high.

The sea breeze was strong, and Hurricane could let himself cruise by mixing gliding and flying. He used his gliding periods to scope out the important areas that Chunk, Lucky, and Crusher had told him about.

Although Hurricane did not know the facts about Bruno da Boss's plot, he realized something would be happening soon between the two gangs, and he was planning his own "where" and "when."

What he saw below was a rush of activity. He saw the Kid leading a group of Bennies along the boardwalk. Big Tuna was working with a group of soldiers setting up hiding places, and Hurricane saw his own soldier, Crusher, watching from the top of the Sky Ride. Finally, he saw Bruno da Boss on the roof of the miniature golf.

Hurricane saw Bruno was watching the activity, too, but he was also directing operations. Hurricane knew the two families would be meeting up for the fight soon, and he wondered how Mack Daddy and Goomba were doing. Hurricane was troubled.

"Goomba should be makin' some defenses, and it worries me I can't see Mack Daddy anywhere. Bruno's enforcer, Tony Ravioli, ain't anywhere either. Now what's up with that?" Hurricane decided he better confront Bruno

to cause a distraction. Plus, Bruno would get suspicious if Hurricane didn't show up to pull his chain.

Hurricane made his approach from behind Bruno's back. He stayed up high to miss being spotted by one of the Benny crew, and then dropped to land next to Bruno on the roof. He saw Bruno give a slight jump as he landed, but Hurricane was impressed at how well Bruno hid his surprise.

"Hey, how ya doin'?" Bruno asked. "I been waitin' for you." Bruno realized Hurricane would be able to see some of his war plans from up on the rooftop, so he flew down in front of the arcade, hoping that Hurricane would follow.

Hurricane took his time, surveying the area from the roof, knowing that it would make Bruno nervous. Although he had already seen most of Bruno's planning from the air, he was using his time on the roof to see if Tony Ravioli was close by. Tony's mission was the part of Bruno's plan that Hurricane did not yet understand.

When Hurricane realized Tony was not there, he flew down to Bruno. "We got some unfinished bizness," he said to Bruno, using his powerful chest to push Bruno back against a wall. Bruno pushed back, knowing his bulk was just as threatening.

"I'm ready for ya. Right now is fine with me," Bruno grunted.

"Hey, Daddy!" a little human cried out. "Look at those seagulls! Are they dancing?" He started throwing his popcorn at Hurricane and Bruno. Suddenly, all the birds in the area began grabbing at the popcorn, starting a feeding frenzy.

"We'll finish this tonight," Hurricane growled.

"Yooze know where to find me. I'll be waitin' right here," Bruno threw back.

Hurricane went winging off to Tom's Diner to meet his crew.

The Showdown

Chunk flew to the FunTown Pier to meet Crusher and Lucky. He spotted Mack Daddy on the ride called the Tower of Fear, and he landed close by.

"I wanted to report to ya that I saw Tony Ravioli feedin' at the salt marsh down the beach. I know you was lookin' for him."

Mack Daddy barely looked at him as he lifted off. "Yeah, thanks." Chunk realized he had made an enemy in Mack Daddy, although he wasn't sure how. Maybe Mack Daddy was jealous of the attention Hurricane had been giving Chunk. Chunk knew he better watch his back. He looked out and saw Crusher and Lucky eating out of a bag on the beach, and he went down with them.

"That's the last time I split up from you two," Chunk told his buddies. "There's some serious attitudes out there, and we better not be out alone. How'd you two do?"

"We found Big Tuna. He's got his guys piling up rocks and seashells in all the hideouts. Looks like those are gonna be their weapons of choice," Crusher stated. "Ya ready to head out to Tom's Diner?"

"Yeah, let's get over there to report," Chunk agreed. A short time later, they landed at the parking lot. Hurricane had already started the meeting, but he waved at the three gulls to come up to the front.

"Whatcha got?" he demanded.

Lucky and Crusher looked at Chunk, so he started answering.

"Well, I heard from some Bennies at the salt marsh that the rumor is Bruno's planning on hittin' us tonight. I also ran into Tony Ravioli down there, and I let Mack Daddy know I saw him."

"Good work," said Hurricane. "I pretty much set the same time with Bruno da Boss a little while ago. Tonight it is. What 'bout you two? Can't ya talk?" He looked at Crusher and Lucky.

"Oh, yeah, boss, we can talk," said Lucky.

Chunk nudged him and then whispered, "Hurricane wants ta know what ya found out!"

"Uh, we saw Big Tuna and his soldiers putting rock and seashell piles together," Lucky explained.

"Huh," said Hurricane. "Ammunition—we'll have to watch out. They'll be flyin' over us and dropping 'em on our heads. Goomba, whut do you got goin'? Any weapons?"

"Sure, boss, I ain't gonna let you down. The boys and me been puttin' together slingshots. We can shoot dose Bennies out of the air!"

"Slingshots! How'd ya do it?"

"We got some of those clothespins off clotheslines. Then we went into the games area in da casino and stole the rubber bands they use to hang up the prizes. We can set up teams and shoot seashells. The clothespin can hold the rubber band, a soldier can hold the clothespin, and a couple other soldiers can load and shoot from the rubber band. Watch, boss, we been practicing."

Hurricane was proud as he watched his crew get into teams and shoot pieces of seashells out of the slingshots. "Smart!" he praised Goomba. "Follow Crusher so he can show ya where Bruno's hideouts are, and get the guns set up in those areas. Lucky, you help Goomba assign our own locations to da teams. Time's runnin' out. Everybody stay in their places until I give Goomba the signal to start the fight."

Hurricane turned to Chunk. "I want yooze to stay with me. Do ya think you can keep up with me and my other guards?"

"Whatever ya need boss!" Chunk responded excitedly.

If Chunk thought he was on his way to the battlefront, he was soon disappointed. Hurricane headed for the beach, and Chunk understood their real goal as soon as he saw the two girls waiting.

Hurricane landed smoothly in front of Dyna and Tracy. "Ready for dinnah, ladies?" he asked. "What's ya choice—a sandwich or our famous Joisey pizza?"

"I always likes to try the local cuisine!" Tracy answered. "Especially Eyetalian!"

Hurricane did not even look at Tracy, waiting for Dyna to reply. "Well, if you is recommendin' the pizza joint, I guess it's worth a try. Where'd ya say it was located?"

"It's over at the Casino Pier. I got a little bizness goin' there later. Come on."

Hurricane let Dyna leave first, catching up to act as her escort. Tracy gave a sigh and took off after them, and Chunk found her flying close to him. Chunk was startled when Tracy began talking to him. Girls just did not do that.

"So, do yooze like this pizza place we're goin' to?" Tracy quizzed.

Chunk could hardly reply he was so panicked, trying to think of the right answer. "I don't know if you can ask me that," he finally said. "I mean, take a look. Ya can tell I don't

say no too much when it comes to food." And he gave his laughing call.

"Yeah, I hear ya. I love to eat, but the guys like a girl who's skinny. I just get to dream about eating," Tracy sighed.

"I like a girl who can fill out her feathers," Chunk said softly, thinking Tracy could not hear him as the group was landing next to the Pier Grill and Pizza shop, but she turned and gave him a smile.

Hurricane set the two girls up on top of an empty picnic table. As they watched, he waited for the young clerks to turn their backs, and then flew onto the counter and picked up a piece of pepperoni and cheese pizza, which he set down in front of them. Dyna and Tracy were impressed at the ease with which he lifted the pizza.

The other birds in the group picked up food from the ground in the surrounding area. Chunk was still dazed from the beautiful smile Tracy had given him and was wandering around the area hoping no one would notice. His thoughts were sidetracked as he saw one of Bruno da Boss's crew.

At first, Chunk was on his guard, thinking the bird was spying on the group, but then he noticed the bird was throwing up. He quietly went over to Hurricane and tried to get his attention. When Hurricane looked at him, Chunk pointed with his wing toward the sick bird.

"Well, little ladies, are ya done chewin'? We can head up to the arcade and see whatsa story up there." He started to move the two girls away from the sick bird, walking toward the other end of the pier.

"What's your hurry?" asked Dyna. "We coulda maybe ate another piece!"

"Yeah, well, there's more to be doin' than just stuffin' our beaks. We ain't done yet." Hurricane was navigating the girls through the vacationing human crowd.

"Look who's talkin'. Who do ya think you are? I don't stuff my beak. My mother came from England. She lived on top of Buckingham Palace. She was one of the queen's birds."

Hurricane turned toward Chunk. "This one's got a mouth on her! I love that in a girl." And he put his wing around Dyna. Suddenly, Hurricane stopped dead, dropping his wing to his side.

Chunk turned and looked up the pier and saw Bruno da Boss with the Kid, Big Tuna, and many of his other soldiers.

Hurricane had thought he was going to be able to choose the time and place of the battle. He realized now that Bruno had beat him to it. He nudged Chunk and leaned close. "It's goin' down. I need Goomba and Mack Daddy now. You find them. Get there fast and get there alone!"

Tracy was surprised as Chunk took off. She had been getting ready to talk to him again. Hurricane turned to Dyna. "Looks like my bizness is startin' a little early. I'm gonna have one of the boys here escort ya back to the beach. If you're interested, I'll look ya up tomorrow." Dyna smiled at him sweetly. "Yeah, that'd be good. Right, Tracy? These guys are busy and want us outta here, like yesterday! C'mon." She flew off without waiting for an escort. Tracy quickly followed her.

Hurricane wondered if Dyna might be angry, but he didn't have time to think about her now. He turned to face Bruno, who was walking toward him down the pier with his family behind him.

Meanwhile, Dyna and Tracy perched on the carousel. Dyna had decided no one was going to chase her out. She was impressed at Hurricane's bravery, as she watched the action. One gull against many. Hurricane standing strong and large.

As Hurricane walked slowly through the vacationing human throng, his eyes never left Bruno's eyes. His crew began to appear from their lookouts and joined him.

Crusher and Lucky were right next to Hurricane, guarding his flanks until Goomba and Mack Daddy showed up.

It seemed as though the humans parted, watching the two groups of gulls approach each other.

Suddenly, a bird descended jerkily from the air, screeching harsh cries, and crashed to the pavement. The bird continued to thrash as though in great pain, and then stopped moving. Many of the humans shrieked, and one person knocked the body toward a trash can.

"That's Jo-Jo!" exclaimed the Kid. "One of our boys!"

By this time, Bruno and Hurricane were nearly face-to-face. "How many of my family is ya gonna erase? What kinda poison is ya usin'?" said Bruno, with a snarl.

"I don't know what you're talkin' about, Bruno," Hurricane answered.

"My guys—they're pukin' their guts out everywhere," said Bruno, "and now Jo-Jo there looks like he's gonna buy the big one."

Just then, Mack Daddy and Goomba flew in, carrying Tony Ravioli, each of them holding one of his wings. Chunk landed with them.

"Hurricane, we found Tony Ravioli real sick like. We didn't think we should just leave a top guy lying on the beach in the surf, so we brought him here," said Chunk.

It suddenly dawned on Hurricane what was going on. "This is what you're accusing me of, Bruno? Ya think I'd use poison like a coward instead of facin' ya in a fight?"

Hurricane went for Bruno's neck, when something hit his side and knocked him off balance. He swung around to attack the new threat when he realized it was Dyna.

Dyna stood between the two bosses, looking very small but determined. "Stop a-ready! You two hafta figure this out. If birds are sick and dying, and it ain't cause of this fighting—well, you are the leaders of these families, ain't ya?"

Bruno and Hurricane looked at each other, and then looked at their crew. They saw fear and shock in the birds' eyes.

Dyna continued her lecture, "This is ridiculous. It's not time to fight. It's time to work together for a solution. Yooze two gotta have a sit-down and have a meetin'."

Hurricane walked over to Tony Ravioli. Bruno followed him. Tony looked up, gasping. "Boss, I hurt bad. I got cramps and keep bein' sick. I can't get up."

Hurricane looked down at the shiny band on his leg and read the writing on it—Manahawkin WMA. He flashed back to when he was flying in the storm, hurricane-force winds throwing him in all directions. His wing seemed to ache again with the pain he had felt when he had hit a

large rock and broken it. Hurricane remembered the humans who had found him and helped heal his wing.

"Bruno, I gots an idea. I think I got someplace we can get answers. Chunk, Goomba, you lift that Jo-Jo bird in your beaks and follow us, he's still breathin'and maybe we can get him help. Crusher, Lucky, grab Tony's wings. We have a long trip ahead of us."

"Why should I listen to some lug?" Bruno asked. "Why do yooze think I'd trust you? You stole my girl." He pointed at Dyna.

Dyna's anger was visible in her eyes. "Your girl? I ain't nobody's girl. But you do have a sick guy here, and ya better figure out how to help."

"Listen, Bruno, whatever this is, it could spread to all of us boyds. Yooze could lose Tony next. This place will help us. They helped me before," said Hurricane.

Bruno sighed. "I shoulda just stayed in bed. I never thought I'd be joinin' up with a goon like you. Let's get goin'. Big Tuna, follow at the tail end."

Bruno and Hurricane took to the air. Chunk and Goomba lifted up the unconscious bird, Jo-Jo, and Crusher and Lucky followed with Tony. Big Tuna and Mack Daddy brought up the rear.

Dyna took to the air after them. "C'mon," Dyna said to Tracy. "They might need some help carryin' those guys."

Hurricane was taking them to the Manahawkin Wildlife Management Area, the refuge for birds. He had been taken there by the humans when they rescued him from the hurricane. The refuge was located farther down the New Jersey coast near Barnegat Bay.

What Hurricane did not understand was that a bird preserve did not only help the endangered birds, but also invited the predators!

It was getting close to dusk when the flock of seagulls reached the edge of the wildlife refuge. The gulls heard bird cries they did not recognize, and then noticed shadows against the sun. One of the shadows began diving toward them. Hurricane reacted immediately.

"Hawks!" he cried. "Mack Daddy, Big Tuna! Come with Bruno and me. The rest of you, head to that bridge and follow the road you'll see. Look for the buildings. Stay hidden by flying using the trees as cover. Let's go, Bruno, we got our fight now—only we gotta fight together!"

As Dyna and Tracy started to head for the woodlands below, the diving hawk changed its course and went after them. "Bruno—stop him! C'mon Mack Daddy and Tuna— let's take on dese goons!"

Bruno sized up the hawk heading for the two girls: it looked like it was focusing on Dyna. The red-tailed hawk's talons were curved to grab, and its sharp-hooked beak was open, ready to cut and tear. Bruno shifted his bulk, expanding his chest as much as possible.

Bam! Bruno pounded into the side of the hawk, catching it by surprise and knocking it away from the girls. "Quick! Don't look back! Follow me!"

Out of fear, Tracy had to look over her shoulder. She screeched a warning as she saw the hawk coming back towards them, targeting Bruno as the biggest threat. "Bruno, Bruno, look out!"

Dyna was flying behind Bruno and looked up as the shadow of the large hawk passed over her. Bruno was trying to reach the trees but the hawk was nearly on him.

Dyna called out to Tracy, "I've got his left—use your beak and the claws on your legs—get him on the right!"

Bruno realized he could not make the trees and maneuvered away from the hawk's direct attack, turning to meet the hawk beak to beak. The two girls changed course and charged the hawk from each side, stabbing their beaks and claws into him.

The three pronged attack severely hurt the hawk's ability to function, and he started falling to the ground. The three seagulls rode him to the ground, inflicting further injury as they went. The speed of the fall caused the hawk to hit the ground heavy, and as the seagulls hovered around him they saw he was no longer moving.

"Great teamwork, ladies," Bruno growled. "You probably saved my life."

Bruno led the girls into the shelter of the treetops and then went skimming the air close to the ground. He saw a shelter of stones ahead and brought the girls to a stop there.

"Plant yourselves here—I hafta go help Hurricane put da screws on those hawks!" And with that, Bruno left.

Bruno shot out of the woods into the sky, just in time to see Hurricane lure one of the hawks over the marsh, then dive into the shallow water so that the hawk overshot its mark.

Hurricane was carefully moving through the grasses, using the twilight to hide. As the hawk cruised over the marsh looking for him, Hurricane exploded up in front of it, gouging at the hawk's eyes with his beak. The hawk let out a bloodcurdling screech as it fell, blinded, into the marsh.

Unfortunately, Mack Daddy was not as lucky. Bruno saw another hawk fly over Mack Daddy and then suddenly fold up and dive in for the kill. Bruno could hear a *snap* as the hawk grabbed and saw Mack Daddy's wing fall useless. The two birds dropped together to the ground, and Bruno lost sight of them in the dark.

He cruised over the marsh, but could find no sign of Big Tuna. "Did the hawks take down two of their best guys?" he wondered.

Hurricane's silhouette was outlined against the last faint red from the setting sun. He was flying slowly toward the woods, and Bruno met him. The two exchanged the bad news of losing Mack Daddy and Big Tuna. Then Bruno took Hurricane to where he had left Dyna and Tracy.

The four seagulls huddled together under the rocks for the night. They were all resting after their fights with the hawks. Hurricane felt guilt and sadness that he

had not been able to help protect his friend and soldier, Mack Daddy.

Hurricane was bleeding in a couple of spots, and Dyna was smoothing his feathers, trying to get the bleeding to stop. Bruno and Tracy could see that the two were becoming more than friends.

Joining Forces

Darkness had fallen over the wildlife refuge, and eleven-year-old Jimmy was yawning with boredom. His father, Dave Reynolds, had brought him to work with him. Dave was a marine biologist and worked sampling the ocean and marsh areas.

Dave had his head bent over a microscope, while Jimmy read a book on his tablet. When his dad talked about his job, he made it seem real interesting. But actually being with his dad all day at the refuge was something else—not nearly as fun as Jimmy had anticipated. "I could have read this book at home *and* played a video game or watched TV," he thought, as he yawned again. He and his dad were the only ones left in the lab.

Suddenly, Jimmy heard a thump against the near window. When he looked up, all he could see was the darkness. "What was that, Dad?"

Dave looked up from the microscope and stared toward the window. He went over to the door and opened it. Light beamed out as the movement triggered a sensor spotlight. Lying on the ground were two seagulls, still showing life as they twisted in agony. Dave went over and examined them more closely, wondering if they had flown into the window and knocked themselves senseless. One of the birds lifted his head and vomited.

"Hold that door, Jimmy!" Dave called to his son as he pulled gloves out of his pocket and put them on. He picked up the two birds, one in each hand, and walked into the lab. As Jimmy went to close the door, four more seagulls flew in, one diving close to Jimmy's head.

"Geez!" Jimmy yelled as he ducked, waving his arms over his head to keep the birds away. The door slammed, and the seagulls flew wildly about the room, squawking and crying out.

"In here, Jimmy," Dave called, pushing through a door that led to an examination room, still holding the two seagulls. Jimmy rushed in after his dad, turning to look back through the door's window. The birds were still flying crazily and screaming.

"They'll settle down, son. They must be part of the flock these two birds came from. How in the world did they get from up the coast to our door?" Dave shook his

head in disbelief. "This is going to make us a little late for dinner. Do you want to help me with these two?"

"Sure!" Jimmy responded. "What can I do?"

"Get some of those clean, sterilized towels and put them on top of the table. Remember to put on a pair of the disposable gloves first."

Jimmy spread the towels on the table and stepped back as his father gently laid the two birds down. "I'll have to take some blood specimens. Jimmy, can you get me a couple of those glass vials on the shelf? Then I'll need your help holding the birds while we put bands on their legs. You can write the band information in the log for me."

Jimmy felt a surge of pride that he could be helpful to his father. Working with the live birds made the day more fun and interesting. After they banded the birds' legs, Jimmy sat down as his dad completed the examinations.

"That's all I can do tonight, Jimmy," he said. "I know there is an infection, but I'll need more information. I don't know if this guy is going to make it, though. He hasn't even opened his eyes and is having trouble breathing." He put Jo-Jo in a cage.

"What about the other one, Dad?" Jimmy asked. "He keeps looking at me so sad like."

"He seems to be a fighter, Jimmy. We'll let him rest tonight and see what we can do in the morning." Jimmy's dad put Tony Ravioli in another cage. "Let's go out the back door so we don't upset the loose birds in the front office. When the rest of the staff comes in, they can help us catch and band them."

"You mean I can come back with you tomorrow, Dad?"

"Sure! I think I'll need you tomorrow. You were a great assistant tonight."

The two left for home, both smiling.

The Humans

When morning dawned, Hurricane, Bruno, Dyna, and Tracy went in search of Goomba's group with the sick gulls, following the route Hurricane remembered, over the bridge and down the road until they spotted the wildlife preserve's station.

Inside the Manahawkin Wildlife Management Reserve, the personnel had been busy catching and tagging the loose seagulls that had arrived the night before, putting them in cages so they would be safe and could be fed. Jimmy and his father had gotten to the refuge early that morning. His dad had been right: one of the sick seagulls was dead. Soon the other wildlife team members arrived: an animal scientist and a veterinarian. They were happy to help with the tagging.

Hurricane flew up to a window ledge and saw Tony Ravioli in the hands of a man in a white coat. Flying around the building, he saw a woman at another window, over a

sink. Hurricane landed on that ledge and pecked at the glass until the woman looked up and saw him. She opened the window and then noticed the band on Hurricane's leg.

"Hey, Dave, here's another seagull, but this one's got one of our bands on his leg." Jane reached for Hurricane, but he evaded her hands and flew into the room, followed by Bruno, Tracy, and Dyna.

"Wow, Dad!" Jimmy said excitedly. "This is like a seagull convention or something!"

"Well, none of the new group seems sick," said Dave, as he watched the birds find perches in the room. He slowly walked over to Hurricane and carefully picked him up. "The number on this band is 36852. Jane, take a look in the log and see when this guy was in here."

Jane was an animal scientist, investigating differences between oceanic fish and farm-raised fish. A short time later, Jane found the entry in the center's log. "That bird was here during the hurricane two years ago. It says he had a broken wing. It's quite a coincidence that all of these seagulls are showing up at about the same time. Do you think he has a relationship with the sick gulls that showed up?"

"Well, I guess anything's possible," replied Dave. "Open the door to the exam room, Jimmy, so these four can see the other gulls. We'll be able to tell if they are part of the same flock by their behavior." Jimmy ran over, opened the door and then stood back out of the way.

Bruno flew up onto the top of the door and looked into the room. He saw Chunk, Crusher, Goomba, and Lucky sitting on perches in a large, caged area. Goomba was rubbing his leg with his beak where a band similar to Hurricane's had been attached. Bruno saw the same bands on Lucky, Chunk, and Crusher. Bruno landed on top of the cage.

"Hey, where's Tony? What'd those humans do with Jo-Jo?"

Hurricane, Tracy, and Dyna flew over to join the other birds. Chunk was just beginning to answer Bruno, "Those humans took Jo-Jo. I gotta tell ya we don't know what went down with him. Tony's over there."

All the birds' eyes followed Chunk's pointing wing and saw Tony in one of the human's hands. She was dropping liquid into his mouth. "Dat's very encouraging!" Bruno laughed. "They figured out how important food is to Tony!"

Dave and Jane walked over to the veterinarian, Natalie, who was holding Tony. Jimmy followed his father and listened as he questioned the vet. "So, after looking inside the dead seagull, you've discovered these birds have been eating infected sea snails?"

"Yes," Natalie replied. "The sea snails they were eating are carriers of a parasite—a flatworm called a fluke. I've

63

just given this gull some medicine to force the flatworms out of him. I am hoping he'll pull through and won't die like the other bird."

"I can't understand what brought these sick birds to us, but whatever it was I am glad it happened," remarked Dave. "We need to find out how far the infection has gone in this seagull population and see if we can find out where these diseased sea snails are located."

As he was speaking, Hurricane dove down toward Jimmy. Jimmy ducked, hollering out. His father watched the seagull's tricks and said, "I think he is trying to land on you. Hold still. That's the bird that was here before—Hurricane."

Sure enough, Hurricane flew downward again and dropped heavily on Jimmy's head, knocking it sideways. "He's heavy!" Jimmy exclaimed, trying to stand quietly. The bird then hopped onto his shoulder and pulled on the bill of Jimmy's New Jersey Devils cap.

The three grown-ups laughed. Dave said, "This guy must be used to being around people. Looks like you have a new friend!"

Natalie was deep in thought. "It's possible these birds can lead you to the location of the infected snails—after all, somehow they found us. We put leg bands on all of them, but even though the band will identify them in

our log, it won't help us follow them. I suggest we put a GPS locator on one of the birds and follow them in the boat."

"Good idea," said Dave. "But which bird?" It was the humans' turn to look at the seagulls sitting in the caging area.

Natalie pointed to Chunk and chuckled. "I think that pudgy guy. He looks like he'd know where to find any food!" Natalie retrieved a small GPS tracker and a new pair of gloves and went into the cage to Chunk. She spoke to him softly, "Come here little guy. This won't hurt."

As Natalie reached for Chunk, he tried to bite her in his fear, but he only got the glove on her hand. She enclosed his wings with her hands and took him out of the cage, leaving the cage door open.

Dave came over to help her attach the GPS to the band on Chunk's leg. The other birds were screaming out harsh alarm cries, and Hurricane and Bruno were flying up to the ceiling to get into attack mode. Jimmy drew back under the cover of one of the counters.

Jane opened all the doors, including the cages and the ones leading outside, and then Natalie let Chunk go free. Hurricane understood what was happening and flew down to lead the birds out.

It was a clear day, and Hurricane circled the edge of the woodlands, keeping away from the marshes and the hawks. Once he saw the ocean ahead, he led the flock of gulls north toward Seaside Heights Beach.

Unknown to the seagulls, the humans had gotten on their boat and were following them along the coast line, watching Chunk's journey on their GPS tracking device. Jimmy was excited to be on the ocean. It was still early in the day, but the sun was not breaking through the clouds forming overhead, and the ocean waves were choppy.

Natalie the vet asked Dave, "Have you received any weather reports today?"

"Well, I forgot to check before we left, but I'm looking at our radar screen here, and I don't see any storm system close. It's just a cloudy day, I guess."

Bruno flew up next to Hurricane. "We got a sayin' in Brooklyn: never leave your buddies behind. Whatta 'bout Tony Ravioli? And I don't even know what went down with Big Tuna."

"Yeah, well I had to leave Mack Daddy behind, and he ain't comin' back. Tony Ravioli will be OK," said Hurricane. "Those humans took care of me until my wing was better and they could let me fly free. We can go back and check on Tony. First we hafta find out what's makin' our guys sick. Turn around, those humans are followin' us. I think dey know somethin'."

Bruno flew up high and behind them and spotted the boat with the humans on it.

"Wow, how'd you know dat?" he asked when he went back to Hurricane.

"I'm always watchin'," Hurricane explained. "These humans takes care of boyds. I seen a lotta different boyds when I stayed with 'em, and lots of 'em were sick. I'm bettin' they're gonna take care of us."

"Chunk!" Hurricane called out. "Get over here." Chunk came up alongside Bruno and Hurricane.

"Chunk, where was Tony Ravioli when you, Mack Daddy, and Goomba found him sick on the beach?"

"He was over by that salt marsh I was tellin' ya about. The one the Kid found to feed the Bennies."

"What was you doin' followin' the Kid?" snarled Bruno.

"All's fair in war, Bruno," said Hurricane. "Don't try to tell me ya wasn't spyin' on us. But this is more important. Take us over there, Chunk."

The humans on the boat were watching their GPS system, which was tracking the flock of seagulls. Natalie noticed Chunk. "Doesn't it look as though our chubby guy is leading the group now? I guess we put the tracking device on the right bird!" she said.

The wind off the ocean had picked up, and the birds were having trouble making progress. Hurricane and Bruno were flying ahead of Tracy and Dyna.

"Hey, Tracy!" Dyna yelled. "Let's use those guy's big bulk for shelter." The two girls laughed as they quickened their pace and caught up to Hurricane and Bruno. They adjusted their flying to stay directly behind the two larger gulls to try to cut down on the wind that was hitting them.

The humans in the boat were also tossing in the waves, and as the clouds kept forming, they were losing sight of the seagulls, depending on their GPS tracker to keep going in the right direction.

Finally, Chunk spotted the salt marsh and landed on the beach. The other gulls followed him. There were several sick and dead gulls lying in the area. Some were Bennies that Bruno recognized, and there were even a couple of Hurricane's Tommies.

"Wow!" Chunk exclaimed. "It looks like this place is cursed. Everybody's kickin' off."

Hurricane grilled Chunk. "You ate here, Chunk. Now think, what did ya eat or not eat?"

Chunk went over to the marshy water, looking down at its inhabitants. "Yeah, well, I had some of dose crabs and a coupla crayfish. I was gonna eat some of those sea snails, but Tony Ravioli chased me off."

Hurricane looked over Chunk's shoulder. "This place is full of dose snails. Knowin' how gulls like snails, I'm thinkin' that's what's knockin' off all our guys."

"Yeah, Tony was eatin' 'em when I took off," noted Chunk.

"Goomba," called Hurricane. "Yooze better go find our soldiers and give them the lay of this place. Find out how many was feedin' here, and if they look sick, we have to get 'em to the humans."

He turned to Bruno. "Hey, Bruno. Is that one of your punks over there? Maybe yooze should send him, too. Your family ain't gonna listen to one of my men. Any boyd we can get to the humans might be saved."

"Quit ya spittin', Hurricane! I ain't one a your goons," Bruno snapped back, but then he went over to one of his crew that was in the feeding area. He told him about the sickness and asked him to follow Goomba to tell the rest of the Bennies.

"Get the sick ones back here!" Bruno yelled as the two birds left.

The wind was whipping up stronger, and the birds watched as the humans' boat struggled through the rough surf. Dave dropped anchor and asked Jimmy to help unload equipment into their rubber dinghy. The four humans got carefully into the small boat as it rocked in the rough sea and headed to shore.

Natalie began examining the sick and dead gulls while Dave and Jane put on boots and waded into the salt marsh.

"Stay here with Natalie, Jimmy," his dad warned. "We aren't sure what we're dealing with yet."

The scientists began picking up sea snail specimens and putting them into jars. Dave cut one open on the beach, and Jane took a video of the area, actually putting the camera beneath the surface of the water.

"Look!" Jane called to Dave. "Watch these snails. You can tell by their behavior that they are infested. They are going upward as the tide is rising. Usually they would move horizontally and down toward the floor of the marsh. This upward movement is making it easier for the gulls to grab and eat them. It's a reaction to the flatworms inside of them."

The two scientists were so intent on their investigation that they were not paying attention to the scene around them.

Natalie, however, was getting anxious. She could barely kneel in the winds, which had picked up power. The wind was pelting her with sand, and she could see many birds in the area beginning to lift off. She looked out and saw the black sky; the huge waves rolling in grabbed the boat up and threw it back down into the ocean. "Jimmy, we've got to get your dad and Jane!"

They ran toward the two scientists. "Quick! We have to find some shelter! Look at what's developing over the ocean."

Dave looked out. "I can't believe it! That tropical storm reported off the coast of North Carolina a few days ago must have moved north! This looks severe—like a hurricane may be developing."

"What are you talking about?" Natalie asked. "Hurricanes don't travel this far north, do they?"

"Well, it's rare," replied Dave, "but not unheard of. The water temperature has been extremely warm, and the conditions in the air may have changed. Hurricanes can travel as far North as New England. I'll see if I can get any tools off the boat to help us shelter. Jimmy, stay with Jane and Natalie." He started toward the ocean, his head down in the strong winds.

FRIENDS IN NEED

"The boat's gone!" Natalie screamed to be heard over the howling wind, as rain began hammering at them. The three humans looked at the ocean. They saw the waves charging at the beach, seeming to reach at least twenty feet high and slamming down closer and closer to them.

Bruno was arguing with Hurricane. "I ain't askin' ya! I'm tellin' ya! We gotta get outta here."

Hurricane was watching the humans' distress. "We can't make it back to Seaside Heights. And we hafta help those humans, too. They saved my life before. I owe 'em, Bruno. Plus they are our only hope to save our crews. I know a place we can all go and be safe. I used it before, when I broke my wing." Hurricane thought about the cave he had dragged himself to when he had been hurt.

He looked around, barely able to see in the darkening skies and heavy rain. He hoped he could find the cave again, to save all of them. He spotted Lucky, Crusher, and

Chunk trying to shield Tracy and Dyna with their wings. "Get ready to shadow me," he yelled at them. "I have a place where we can get outta this storm."

Hurricane turned back to Bruno. "Help me get the humans' attention. We need to make them move."

The two seagulls flew over to the humans; Hurricane landed on Jimmy's head, and Bruno started grabbing at coats and hair and then flying a short distance away. The humans fell to the ground, thinking the gulls were attacking them. Hurricane and Bruno came back repeatedly, grabbing the humans' clothing, flying away, and then flying back.

Jimmy realized the birds were not trying to hurt them. "Dad!" he yelled out. "I think they want us to follow them."

The wind was raging loud and hard by now, and the rain made it hard to see or move, nearly drowning them with its force. All of the birds were struggling to follow Hurricane, but the strength of the storm was too much for Tracy and Dyna, and they dropped to the beach.

Natalie nearly fell over them, and then she scooped up both Tracy and Dyna and sheltered them in her lab-coat pockets. Hurricane, with the other gulls, flew ahead until they were lost to sight.

Dave struggled forward. A small outcrop of rocks came up, and he hunched against them, consulting his GPS and its directional readout as closely as he could in the torrential rain.

He went to wrap his arm around Jimmy to support him through the storm, but Jimmy wasn't there! Dave tried to see around him, but the strength of the wind was lashing the rain and sand into his eyes. "Jimmy! Jimmy!" he screamed, but his words were blown back to him, and he knew they would not be heard.

Natalie and Jane joined with him, screaming Jimmy's name together, and suddenly Hurricane appeared and landed on Dave's shoulder pulling at him. "No, no! Jimmy is missing!" Dave yelled throwing his arm toward the shore.

Hurricane lifted off Dave to go looking for Jimmy. The wind pushed him down and his belly hit the sand—hard. Then it sucked him up, spiraling. Hurricane was afraid he would not make it out of another storm alive, but he knew he had to keep trying. He pointed his body into a dive, pushing outside the spiral, and was able to stabilize.

He saw a moving shadow to his right and flew in that direction. It was Jimmy, stumbling on the beach and shouting feebly for his father.

Hurricane landed on Jimmy's back, and Jimmy turned with a look of fear that soon changed to a smile and yell of happiness. Hurricane flew low to the ground, following the humans' path to the rock outcrop, realizing the path was getting fainter as the wind and rain moved the sand. He kept returning to Jimmy, trying to keep him on course.

Jimmy dropped to the sand in exhaustion. Hurricane landed on him, pulling at his clothes to try to get Jimmy to get up.

Meanwhile, Natalie thrust Dyna and Tracy at Jane, and ran out into the storm trying to follow Hurricane. Squinting against the heavy downpour, her eyes searched the beach as she stumbled along. She was just about to give up her pursuit of the boy and the gull as hopeless when she saw movement.

Natalie moved in that direction, and found a new strength when she realized it was Jimmy and Hurricane. Reaching Jimmy she helped him to stand and pulled her lab coat over their heads, trying to gain herself some visibility. Pushing forward, she followed Hurricane, knowing that was their best hope.

Finally the two fell against the rocks. Hurricane flew to where Jimmy's dad waited with Jane, both of them still hoarsely calling Jimmy's name.

Jimmy and Natalie heard his father and Jane calling, and they called back. Dave rushed up and hugged his son against him. He then turned to hug Natalie, pulling the two of them deeper into shelter. Jane reached for Natalie,

"What were you thinking?" She asked as she hugged the woman. I thought all of you were gone!"

Once again, Hurricane pulled on Dave's coat. Dave realized the wind had picked up to where it was penetrating even their rocky formation and he gestured for all of them to follow the gull. Soon they saw a cave-like indention in the rock. Dave pushed Jimmy and the two women in ahead of him, and they all fell thankfully into the shelter Hurricane had found for them.

Dave took both of Natalie's hands: "How can I thank you for bringing Jimmy safely back to me! I have never seen such courage!"

"I wasn't thinking," Natalie responded. "I just couldn't leave Jimmy out there—I kept thinking I would want someone to find my son! Plus, I didn't do it alone." Natalie smiled as she turned to look at the group of seagulls.

"Hurricane helped save me, Dad!" Jimmy said.

"That seagull has saved all of us I think, Jimmy," replied his father.

Natalie helped Jane take Dyna and Tracy out of her pockets and placed them next to the other birds roosting on the cave wall.

The storm continued to build in power and noise outside the little refuge, and Dave got up and tried to look

out. The darkness outside, combined with the heavy rain and wind, made it nearly impossible. He was worried as he saw water foaming around the rocks in front of the cave. Would the storm surge reach them here?

Hurricane looked back at the humans, shaking his head that they were all sharing the same refuge. He leaned against Dyna. She realized he was exhausted. Finally, Hurricane pulled himself upright and looked to make sure all of the gulls were OK. He smiled to see Chunk with his wing protectively around Tracy—he had never expected that!

Suddenly, water began to fill the cave floor, washing over the feet of the humans. Dave explored the cave and saw a high shelf near the back. "Come here," Dave said to the two women, as he helped Jimmy up. "I found us higher ground!" The women climbed up with them.

"No one will ever believe this story," Jimmy said. The humans looked across at the seagulls roosting with them.

"I'm here and I hardly believe it—saved by seagulls!" responded Dave.

Jane pulled some granola bars out of her pockets, giving one each to Jimmy, Dave, and Natalie and breaking several others up on the rocky shelf for the flock of gulls. The birds flew over to eat, and the group munched quietly hoping the storm would subside.

Finally, it grew quiet, and the water stopped rising. Dave went outside to look around. The sky was clearing, and he could see the storm moving back out to sea.

Hurricane and Bruno left the cave also and knew instinctively it was safe. They sounded their harsh calls to the other birds, who followed them out. "Back to da Casino Pier!" Hurricane told them. "We gotta check on our families."

The flock started to fly inland toward the piers, and Jimmy called out, "Good-bye!" He waved until he lost sight of them.

The group of seagulls flew over Seaside Heights: the Casino Pier was nearly totally destroyed, leaving only part of the damaged roller coaster sticking out of the ocean waves. It appeared that many of the rides and buildings had been smashed by the winds, and at first Hurricane and Bruno had a hard time finding their families.

They both laughed when they saw the two crews roosting together on top of Lucky's Arcade, fighting over bags of chips that had fallen out of a broken snack machine.

"Go figure!" said Bruno. "I thought I came to fight and instead ended up at a party. Really, I never could decide if I wanted a vacation or a fight on this trip."

"I don't mind bankrollin' your vacation, Bruno. I consider myself lucky to know ya," Hurricane answered. The two bosses chest bumped.

Hurricane heard a shout and turned to see Goomba coming out of the arcade. "Hey, boss! We got the sick boyds down here."

Hurricane and Bruno's crews spent the rest of the day getting the sick birds to the beach, where the humans were waiting for another boat to come and pick them up. Hurricane rode on Jimmy's shoulder. Jimmy was glad the bird had come back.

Hurricane watched and saw the veterinarian, Natalie, was giving all the sick birds good care, and also noticed Jimmy's dad was making plans to clean up the salt marsh.

Bruno flew over. "You're a stand-up guy, Hurricane. We hafta be getting' back to Brooklyn after I check on Tony. I'm gonna leave the Kid with him and my other sick guys."

"Yeah, Bruno, ya got nerve. I respect that. This was a good time. Hope ya come back next year."

"Hey, it works both ways—we got stuff goin' in Brooklyn. Consider this an open invitation." Bruno threw his wing around Hurricane, gave him a friendly shove and took off.

Dyna and Hurricane stood together watching as the Bennies flew away. Hurricane turned to face her. "I'm not gonna hafta say good-bye to you, am I? I'm thinkin' we work pretty good together."

Dyna looked out over the ocean where Chunk and Tracy were flying and fishing. Then she looked back at Hurricane, smiling. "I think the Tommies got two new members," she said.

Hurricane and Dyna stood together on the beach as the humans left to go back to the Manahawkin Wildlife Management Reserve. Jimmy and his dad waved good-bye to the birds, and Hurricane rose up, flapping his wings in reply. He realized he had made many incredible friends this summer and found himself smiling at how great that was.